Yes,

I still love

You.

DARSHIT KANGAD

Woven Words Publishers OPC Pvt. Ltd.

Registered Office:

Vill: Raipur, P.O: Raipur Paschimbar,

Dist: Purba Midnapore, Pin: 721401,

West Bengal, India.

www.wovenwordspublishers.in

Email: editor@wovenwordspublishers.in

First published by Woven Words Publishers OPC Pvt. Ltd., 2017

Copyright© Darshit Kangad, 2017

NOVEL

IMPRINT: WOVEN WORDS LAUNCHPAD

ISBN 13: 978-93-86897-16-9

ISBN 10: 9386897164

Price: $10/₹150

Printed and bound in India

CHAPTER 1

Dream

01 May 2016

I was so much happy, life has given me a new tragedy, diverted to a totally different track. I have always dreamt to go abroad and finally, I have started for it...IELTS (INTERNATIONAL ENGLISH LANGUAGE TESTING SYSTEM) was the first step towards it. Everything was dependent on my score in the IELTS exam.

I thought that was not so difficult although everyone denied it but only one person in the world trusted me and that was. my mom. She was my life before life happened! I convinced my parents that I wanted to go abroad, specially to go CANADA, and not to go BANGLORE. My mom supported me and instantly paid me twelve thousand five hundred and ninety-five rupees12,595. It was nothing because, if I had planned for Bangalore it would have costed much. I was sure enough that my taxi fare would have been more than the amount of money required for admission. cost would go only on car expense for admission. Anyways, I knew that money was for my IELTS test. When I went to the IELTS centre, they asked me to sign up a form and then after making the payment, they gave me a receipt and said to visit centre with the receipt between 4pm to -6pm and meet Sheetal ma'am. I didn't understand by the first experience that something was going wrong. Unfortunately, Sheetal ma'am was absent on the very first day of mine. I entered the centre at 2nd floor, there it was written in bold letters ""REMOVE YOUR SHOES OUTSIDE. 100RS FINE APPLIES.",

I was in deep thought and I entered the office with shoes. Hard, rough voice shocked me! "Remove your shoes."

"Oohh! Sorry," I apologized instantly. She was the IELTS faculty and I was lucky that I was not supposed to study in her batch. One madam smiled at me, I guess she was older than my mom. She informed me to talk to Ankita ma'am on the first floor who was giving grammar classes.

I moved downstairs where mam was teaching students in an air-conditioned classroom. Of course, they were grabbing their twelve thousand five-hundred and ninety-five rupees for it. I gestured the teacher to come out; she gave me a supporting look and came out.

"Hello ma'am! Good afternoon... I greeted her with an innocent smile.

"Good afternoon! Are you a new student?"

"Yes, I am and I was instructed to show this receipt to Sheetal ma'am but she is not available today."

"Okay, come in you may sit in my class, we are learning grammar now."

Boom!!!! I entered the class, it was well furnished. There were windows on right side and white board in the centre, a corner was fixed for the computer screen and the table where all stuffs like markers and dusters were used to be there. Wooden benches with soft base were half of full with students. First, I took my seat and then I looked here and there for a while, in the meantime, ma'am was talking to some faculty members upstairs. Oh my God!!! The class was full of boys. The only one girl in the class was there sitting on the first bench. The teacher came in and started giving lecture about "speaking" by asking some questions. She told us about the rules. She also warned us not to talk in our mother tongue. We would be fined ten rupees for speaking in Gujarati, twenty rupees for not having a lead pencil and thirty rupees if someone's cell-phone rang or vibrated during the class. The collected amount would which was supposed to go into a box named "chocolate box" and ultimately would be used for charity.

She asked me to introduce myself in front of whole class. I was nervous and gave a normal introduction, which was obvious, but she taught me how to give an introduction as per IELTS guidelines.

I took a back seat and she asked me questions "Do you think, the way of celebrating festivals has changed from past?"

I answered normally, "Yes it has totally changed, people in past preferred to stay at home and enjoy the festival but now- a- days, they visit other cities and countries so. Bla bla bla...." All other students gave me a look like I had answered a question at the "'KON BANEGA CROREPATI" question correctly and won one1 crore rupees. The ma'am asked me couple of questions that day to analyze my level of knowledge and understanding.

It was 5 O' clock and we were supposed to have a break for five minutes. I thought that everyone would enjoy gossiping but group of boys in groups moved upstairs to drink water and had some chit chats. I thought to go upstairs but no sooner did I move out of the classroom than all other students entered the classroom followed by the teacher, so... again it was a flop idea!!! Time went by speedily like the metro train and soon, it was 6 O' clocks and as soon as ma'am said that 'you may leave' all flew away as if they were caged like birds and they wanted to feel the heights of the sky. But I had no options, I had to waited for my dad and as soon as he came I left the centre.

02 May 2016

Sometimes when everything goes perfectly right in the middle of a boring life, you feel the eagerness to do your best. It was 3:30pm I packed my bag, took my cell phone and wallet as usual and left for my classes. It was now a bit comfortable for me to enjoy my IELTS life. I sat on the second last bench of the middle row alone., After sometime, I realized there was a guy who was sitting alone on the second last bench of another row. I thought I should talk to him and I began with a "Hello!!! What's your name?"

"Harshit," he answered.

"Darshit?" I didn't hear it properly so I asked it once again.

"No, it's Harshit."

"Ok, may I sit there beside you?"

"Oh yes, of course." he firmly replied.

I was not aware about the rules of the classroom, the faculties, the students, and the teaching pattern too.

Ma'am was not there yet in class and we were talking to each other. Two guys came and took their seats. They were best friends so they were gossiping and commenting on various things with each other. Ma'am entered the class and one of that two guys gave a look at her and appreciated her beauty. All who had heard and watched him gave a shy smile and controlled their emotions. Ma'am might have heard their comments too so she inquired what the joke was about. Everybody skewed themselves in silent mode. They started their batch with me and both were students from Marwari families; they were interesting guys and they were too supportive and friendly.

The class began and were in fresh mood as the students were new and ma'am also behaved politely with everyone. As usual there was a break of five minutes! One very smooth and decent voice was heard "Hey bro, give me your number, I'll add you in group" He was Bhavesh. I gave him my number, He was quite different, I knew that he would be my company forever but I kept my emotions and thoughts in control and then we moved in to the class after the break.

At that day, I came to know that there were only two girls in my batch, one was married and another one was engaged, she was Amber, a very good friend and a mad girl. In general, we could use the word 'Psycho' instead of her name! Jokes apart she was very kind-hearted and honest girl I had ever met. Although that didn't matter because I was not interested in that type of thoughts, I had never thought of loving anyone other than my mom, so again we were there to learn and have fun not to find girls. As usual we left at 6 O' clock with great passion of learning ENGLISH. Life was going on so easy and I had not expected that soon it would take a sharp turn!

03 May 2016

Everything was going perfect, I was enjoying my life. Classes were good enough to learn ENGLISH. I was enjoying their teaching pattern. I was regular in my homework. Slowly I began to mix up with other students as well. It was not IELTS main batch so, we didn't have that much good English level and we were not yet serious about the level of IELTS even we were not aware that situation was going to be difficult day by day.

12 May 2016

I reached the classes in advance and we were sitting in parking as usual I was not aware about the tragedy that was going to happen with me and was going to change my life, me, my personality, my surroundings, my ideology, everything in my life. We entered the class after asking permission from ma'am to come in although we had already entered the class. I sat at second last bench of part in front of computer. Ankita ma'am started giving the lecture and nothing new was going to be taught that day as that was an ordinary day which was going to be special for me. I was participating partially in the lecture because it was becoming boring day by day and just after few minutes, my eyes were stuck at something like the thirst for water in a desert, or fire in winter or shade in summer!!! Let me be precise, I saw a girl sitting on the 3rd last bench near the window. Oh my God! I felt like yes, she was the one and I was not going to lose her anyhow. Ma'am asked her for introduction as usual and it was like a routine for us to hear the introduction of new students. She gave her introduction and I focused only on her name "Nency" and I assumed internally that she was an 'Ahir' (of my caste), however, that didn't matter for me. I controlled my emotions along with my words and continued admiring her with silly smile. I was lost somewhere else in the sky and I really didn't remember what ma'am taught that day.

CHAPTER 2

Love at first sight

"Yes, now the story is going to change its direction so get ready"

I was thinking only and only about her as I had never ever flicked through any girl in this world. I had a common group with my two school buddies as we interacted with each other for everything, be it small or big. "Ram" was the name of the group, which included me, Monik, the all-time favourite and supportive guy, good looking and not a believer of Love but he believed in time pass relationships. Another one was Nishant, simple, cut-shot personality, he always liked to be straight to the point but bit popular than us in the matter of girls. I texted in a group - "Hyy guys, good news! New girl in class, she is awesome yaar and I think she is also Ahir, I want to propose her anyhow but I don't have her number."

Both replied instantly, "Congo...Congo... dk." They acted like I had proposed her and she said 'yes.'

"Don't act like she has accepted my proposal."

"So, what? She'll accept it soon, don't worry." Nishant said. We talked on that a lot and they suggested me some tips as they had already passed through it and we slept @ 1/1:30 AM, that was normal for us after 12th board exams they both continued and I left the conversation by wishing them " GOOD NIGHT".

13 May 2016

As it was going to be a great time I prepared myself to be super cool, I reached my class as usual with my dad ten minutes early. We were having chit chats with each other in the parking lot but she didn't come suddenly. We went upstairs and then she came back. Ankita ma'am informed her to sit beside Amber. They both became good friends and Nency called her 'Big sister.' Everything was going perfect and she started mixing up with all of us but still something was missing, her WhatsApp number. As per my knowledge, no love story could survive without social media in 21st century.

23 MAY 2016

Finally, the moment came, which I was waiting for a long time. We were sitting in the class and after the break of five minutes, we were supposed to take our seats. Ma'am was busy upstairs and I sat on the bench and she was next to me. I started conversation from name and it took a twist to caste and trust me guys no one in my life gave me such a big surprising expression after hearing my caste. She said "Tu Ahir Chho"? (You are an Ahir?) and I was like 'Yes I am an Ahir' I'm not lying. Surprisingly it stuck into my mind that Yes, that was the situation where I could go for it. Firmly, as a good boy I said, "Give me your number." Firstly, as a common factor of girls, she gave a childish look and said "Don't give it to anyone else."

"Yes, I'll not give to anyone," I said giving her a look. Ma'am entered the class and we scattered and settled down here and there.

As soon as the class finished, I went downstairs, I thought that they would be waiting for me and as expected they were late, after few minutes when Nency left, three of them (Parth, Monik and Nishant) came as they were trying to find me from a long time. "Bhabi kidhar hai?" They shouted. I gave them a dirty look but I know they were not going to get me; I informed them "she left" in a common

Indian student's manner with some exotic words. We disappeared as it was too late; time ran even faster when we all were together.

8:00 PM, I was having nothing to do and I got her number #Life became interesting. With a great excitement and enthusiasm, I sent her a message "Hii"

She replied me, "hii."

I asked surprisingly, "How come you know it's me?"

She said "Avu dp tara siva biju kon rakhi sake." (who can keep such photos in display picture other than you?)

'Hahaha' it was my profile picture with a gun in one hand and mobile phone in another sitting in a car. She asked, "Is that gun yours?"

I said, "Yes." And she created a scene of joke by commenting that it was not real it was a toy. I sent her 2, 3 more clicks of the same gun to make her realize that it was real and not a toy. We continued our conversation as long as we could. Slightly it was going to be off track and more romantic every minute. As I had kept all my feelings of flirting safe and secure for my very first girl it was going perfect. While coming back to the introduction part, she asked her dad about my grandfather and she texted me that 'you all are dangerous my dad told me, not completely just little bit sometimes.'

I covered back, "Don't lie to me, you all are like that completely,' and it was like going difficult to explain that history was something that we left behind but still name of my grandfather was much popular, somehow, I tried to say that it was my grandpa and me and my dad were totally different. Peacock's eggs were not coloured sentence from her that provoked me to change the topic.

Bunches of messages in Ram. Monik and Nishant were waiting for me to text and I sent them screenshots of her display picture. They never skipped a point to irritate me, and they started with "Ohooo" and all that. Monik started typing "Dk Nency dk Nency" and trust me he wrote approximately hundred times. I left the conversation and started dreaming.

CHAPTER 3

Proposed a girl for the first time

24 MAY 2016

My life was going with an ease. I was creating new relations and I thought it would not harm my old ones but I was totally wrong. Which I came to know, as the time passed away but "put first things first" so let me focus the story around my Love.

VIEC also included new faculty for grammar students. Shweta madam's English was as good as her looks and nature. She was friendly enough to make all of us enjoy learning. There was an activity to be done that day in class that was debate. Ma'am divided all of us into groups and co-incidentally we were in same group and interaction between me and Amber started from there. Amber was in another team. I strongly opposed Amber's points and that created a scene between us and I helped Nency to speak up at least one point as it was compulsion. I fought with Amber indirectly and then directly in short break on that debate topic only and that became our routine we kept going on with small topics and that pushed us into a good Friendship. We both were having fun with small and sweet fights but main focus in my life was that girl Nancy was driving me crazy. I was thinking about her all time. I was thinking for the perfect time to propose her and it was my first time so I was bit nervous. I could easily flirt with any girl but when it came to serious relations, I was two steps back from any other guy.

"I had written some words in my book which would help anyone to increase their vocabulary," she demanded that book from me after class and I introduced Parth, Nishant and Monik to her and then she asked me for that book and I provided with smile and eyes in which unsaid words were flowing banks to banks. All three of them were standing quietly, I thought they believed that the first impression was last impression. She left all of us throwing a sweet good bye.

Suddenly, strong and hard voice came from the back "Aaaa dk," I looked back there was no one. Again, a same voice shouted my name and I looked at 2-3 guys waiting for turn near a Xerox shop. I went near the shop and found my friends. They were shouting and they commented as they have watched me and Nency together. I tried to take it back and created a scene to show them that we are just friends.

I went home, grabbed my phone as usual after relaxing myself with tea and snacks and started texting folks on my phone. I opened my WhatsApp and zoomed…!!! My "hii" message swirled like hurricane to her cell phone. We started chatting, I firmly asked "What are you doing??? "She said that she was going to the shop to repair her ring. There came a new tragic movement from me! I thought that was the best moment to go on, I sent her a ring on WhatsApp and asked "Will you marry me???"

She replied, "Are you serious?" With some emoji which irritate me too much.

"Really yar what's the need of emoji in serious matters." I tried to explain that "Yes, I really wanted to marry her."

She replied me and said that there was something before marriage.

I texted, "Gf? Then will you be my Gf?" As all the girls in the world did, she also asked for time to think. I didn't want to spoil our friendship and I didn't wanted to go in front of her with pending proposal so I tried my best to force her to answer on the spot but I was not able to do that. She said that she would reply till 30th May and I didn't have any choice but to wait for her reply.

Hopefully my result of 12th grade was on the head. It was to be declared anytime. I listed a point to make her feel emotional, she asked my seat number and I provided her with my seat number. It was time to sleep and I took my favourite place i.e. my bed and started dreaming of her. On the other hand, I pinned all the chat in "Ram" they suggested me to keep calm and gave me motivation by saying that she will surely say a "Yes!" How could anyone trust their best friends in the matter of love that's the reason why people actually fall in love, they don't trust their friends.

26 MAY 2016

I was in a deep confusion; weird thoughts were roaming around my mind. I was thinking that if I had done something wrong, it would harm our friendship. Likewise, Bhavesh was aware about things happening around me. He was the one who were motivating me to never give up on the people you love.

With a strong heart, partly wet eyes, silent mood and patience I reached the classroom. She sat slightly on the back of my bench. She tried a lot but I didn't look back, even in short break I didn't talk to her, didn't look at her. I was not able to do so, I felt guilty. We ran out of the building as soon as the class finished. She wanted to talk to me but I stood up with Kunal and Ravi. She shouted "Darshit..."

I went close to her to listen what she wanted to say me, she said "What were you saying yesterday?"

Seriously, I was like 'she didn't take serious what I said.' Few minutes later, my dad came to pick me up. I introduced my dad to her with hand gestures and told her that he was my dad; her tongue came out of her mouth with a cute smile and expression full of fear. I remembered the point and said, "Look at him, he looks dangerous?"

She said, "No not at all." I left the conversation and came home with my dad.

My behaviour seemed changed but my family members didn't remark it. I was a bit stressed; they thought it was due to my examination results.

Days from 26-30 May passed normally like I was waiting for her answer. Unfortunately, I was not able to look at her at class, she tried couple of times but I didn't give her a look.

CHAPTER 4

Step ahead of ordinary life

30th MAY 2016

"ONE OF THE WONDERFUL DAY"

That day's lectures were boring, not because of the faculties but I was not much involving in activities that day. Somehow, ma'am finished the lecture and instructed us to leave. We moved downstairs, as usual as I was talking with Ravi and she was waiting for me! She said that she was going to the main office and I said that I too had a call from ma'am to meet Malhar sir, so, we decided to go together, of-course, not in the same vehicle.

We reached the office. One of my friend, Sidharth sir was there. We had a talk with him and she waited outside for me and I moved towards the office. As I moved inside, the very first face above me was Tanvi ma'am, who never skipped a chance to irritate students. I sat on the chair near Rachna mam's table and Malhar sir instructed me to try in multiple countries and he gave me time to think on it. We left the class after grabbing some more information from Siddharth sir.

We reached the Indira circle and I was supposed to take a right turn but she said to come straight and I agreed. We moved together for some time and then she asked to stop the bike and find a safe place where we could sit and talk. We accelerated our vehicles in one small street and located a sanctum. She asked me for one reason to say me yes for the relationship and I provided lots of it (#overacting bhi zarori he.) I said that I loved her. She counter argued that we have been talking from just couple of days and how it was possible that I fell in love with her? I replied with a smile that love happened like that only and threw another reason that we were of same caste. She remained quiet for some time and then I asked for a reason to disagree! She said that she didn't have any reason to deny my proposal but she was nervous that what if her family came to know about us! I tried to explain that it would not happen and if it would happen, I would marry her legally with the permission of my family.

"Boom, she said yes and we just went home after a hand shake"

I was eager to tell someone and I thought about Parth. His home was in my way so I called him instantly and gave him the good news! He congratulated me and I headed home as usual. I rode my bike at 90-100 kmph and reached home safely.

Folks tell me that I ride too fast but I ride fast only when I was happy or when I was sad but that time I was of course happy. And in my everyday life, I always found a reason to be happy but latter on it converted into a reason to be sad, it happened, it was life, guys, we fall, we cry, we laugh, we become sad, we love, we care, we fight but "We live." To learn all these it took most of my happiest moments which converted into guilt and sadness.

8:00 pm (WITH FAMILY SITTING OUTSIDE IN OPEN AIR)

I created a scene adding Malhar sir's points with extra salt and spice on it and explained that Australia was better than Canada in many ways. They took my points legible and allowed me to go for it. I was so happy and everything was going perfectly right in the middle of confusing life.

31 MAY 2016

"I HAD A GREAT SLEEP"

Last night I had a great sleep because when we get exactly what we want, we feel relaxed and calm enough to enjoy your days and nights. Something happened that we had never imagined but somehow it happened and we didn't have any regrets related to that.

"LAW OF GRAVITATION IS NOT RESPONSIBLE FOR PEOPLE FALLING IN LOVE"

CHAPTER 5

First ever relationship

8 JUNE 2016

"Days passed out like wind I think I was not giving that much love because it was my first time and I was feeling shy even when we were alone."

We attended a seminar by Transglobe. It was for the direct entry into Universities and Colleges. First, we met at Kalawad Road and then moved together in different vehicles. Nishant was supposed to come with us but he was busy with his uncle so we moved without him. I was aware about all of her habits, her likes and dislikes. As soon as we reached The Imperial Palace: the venue, she gave me an innocent look and said that she was thirsty. I took out a bottle of Thumbs Up from my bag which I had kept for her. She gave me a smile and we took a few sips and then looked for the parking space. All the parking place was chargeable and trust me I was not going to pay bucks for such a silly thing and that too to morons. I called one of my childhood friend Hariom, who was the then owner of Hariom Sarees and asked to park my vehicle near his shop, which was located exactly opposite to the venue. We moved our vehicle there, parked it and I informed Hariom about that.

Here we go…

We went inside and a ma'am informed us to sit in the waiting queue. I knew we might have to wait so I had already carried our Priority cards beforehand. We moved in and there came the part one of the high-lightening tragedy.

"Navitas" the leading name under which many students made their career and that day it was represented by Mr. Kuldeep.

First, I was given a form, which we filled outside, trust me guys he gave me a very surprising look by having a glance at my scores! It was as if I had submitted a duplicate passport and he was a visa officer. He gave me a sad look and said that it was not possible to enrol me for Navitas, and then I was waiting for her turn. She was submitting her documents and I was looking at him and he informed me to wait outside. I was not disturbing them! Well, I moved outside and looked around other applicants. She came outside with a huge sparkling smile on her face. I asked, "What happened?" and she said that they could give her admission and we moved outside.

She asked me we could go somewhere because we had 2-3 hours left, we were having class at 4 O' clock so she kept her Activa there and we moved in my bike. We went to the galaxy cinema to check out movie shows but if we go for that we would be late for the class so it was a flop idea. I called Nishant and asked to come at racecourse garden. We sat there and talked to each other and passed the time. Seriously, I was not aware about such expressions from old folks when a boy and a girl visited the garden together.

We sat together and trust me guys; environment was so irritating. People were coming and asking for charity like they were indirectly forcing everyone and begging, oh my god!!! I controlled my temper in front of her and behaved well. Come on guys, I am mature enough to go to a garden with a girl! Sorry not a girl I must say, but a girlfriend.

She became busy with someone on her cell, talking with her friend and roaming here and there and I was admiring her beauty with throwing bottle of cold drinks from one hand to another and then she came towards me with a cute smile, we both were feeling nervous, specially me. my life didn't give me such group ever because I had not done my schooling from a co-educational schooling system.

We had already informed Nishant to join us and we were waiting for him. Nency used her brain to guess who was Nishant, from the people visiting the garden. Unfortunately, she didn't find him and finally he came with a totally different look with a black and red T-shirt with a hat of his grandpa which created an extraordinary scene above us. We sat for some time and he suggested playing teenagers favourite game "Truth and dare." Nency denied for some time and we were an expert in begging for something with excuses which were never legible. Then also somehow, we did it and we started for it.

Game was going with a smooth breeze no one was asking for 'dare' and then Nishant pointed that as a rule of game that you can't stick to the 'truth' only, we were not left with any other choices. It was a dare and she was supposed to ask the name of a child playing with mud and sand along with begging and she accepted the dare, his name was Gopal. Next dare was to Nishant and it was completely funny and insane, he was supposed to act like a mad woman near the fountain and he did it not do it exactly but it was alright. Nishant was smart enough to create something which could neglect space between me and Nency. He threw a dare to me and it was about 'the best feeling in the world' i.e. 'hugs.' I moved further with a smile but she denied because there were too many folks hanging out specially aged ones. We kept that for the time when we would get a perfect chance. Next dare was to ask people who went at the end of garden that what they are exactly doing there and Nency was supposed to record that in her phone as a proof as we were not going with her at the end of garden. They were friends and were just sitting there nothing else. Next dare was for me to ask a boy who was roaming here and there that what he was doing and why he was roaming here and there continuously. She was coming with me to supervise me! What the hell was that as soon as we reached to him, he slept on the grass. I woke him up and asked and finally completed my dare.

"PROMISE IN THE FORM OF DARE"

I got a dare to propose her and Nishant was going to capture that I did it and we decided that whenever we moved back to that place in future I would propose her in the same manner no matter how old we get.

We had lots of fun and "HUG" @ garden was not my cup of tea so I just took her in my arms when we were moving outside. It was time to move because we were having class so we moved towards our class and Nishant went home. We parked our vehicles and as usual the folks were waiting for each other, she moved upstairs and I started with the buddies.

"Whhooofff!!! that was the day when I exactly realized how romantic it was to be with someone, Life was 100% perfect."

Finally, 1 week and 2 days completed of my first ever relationship.

CHAPTER 6

Fun together

14 JUNE 2016

"QUITCHES IS A PART OF ALMOST ALL THE COUPLES OF RAJKOT"

Fun, food, love, romance! (food paragon i.e. cheese grill veg. sandwich)

24 JUNE, 2016

"As you move deep into a relationship, you enjoy more and learn something new every day and you dream something common every day."

"FOR ME THAT WAS A SANCTUM WITH HER, WITHOUT ANY RESTRICTIONS NOTHING ELSE."

We were just in the middle of start of a cute relationship so we had many things to do but less time to arrange everything, may be not for her but for me cause my home was about half an hour run with bike from her. So, we didn't get much leisure time to romance. Finally, we got a common excuse to meet each other i.e. Library. We met each other with an excuse of going to the library instead we visited the class.

"Small fights, lots of feelings, hangout, long drive @new ring road, fun, "Heart to heart connection," was the best part of my teenage, live, love, free, trust, fun, joy, no fear, feeling shameless, #words from personal DIARY."

25 JUNE 2016

Next day was Bhavesh's birthday and we were planning to go to purchase a gift for him. I left Bhavesh at half of the way. We went to the crystal mall @DMART she asked me to try some shirts and she was the first girl other than my mom and sis to judge me in the matter of clothes. I was feeling happy like she was looking at me and giving supportive looks and expressions. Ultimately, we choose a blue shirt for buddy and left for home.

26 JUNE 2016

I woke up early but it took more time to get ready and I was supposed to reach @CCD with gift wrapped and packed properly I was having my tea and both of them reached there I locked the zips of my bag, took a shirt in one bag and started my legend ROYAL ENFIELD 350 (1967) #grandpa's gift and it took eighteen minutes in which we reached stationary after filling petrol at petrol pump, it would be sixteen and half minutes if I would go on my bike and forty-five minutes if my dad was driving the vehicle. Many children were roaming around stationary for books so it took more time to pack the gift.

I was about 1 hour late and she gave me a look they both were sitting and we enjoyed that day with cuisine and best wishes for each other.

God always saved me! I forgot key the in my bike with ignition on and no one had even touched it. I think bullet had its own fame!!!

30 JUNE 2016

"YES, MY LIFE WAS NOT MEANINGLESS"

We all have that one person in our life in whose absence our existence seems utterly meaningless. For some people that one person was their friend or a family member, depending on you instead of being forced into liking and for me that one person was Nency especially just for that time.

Finally, one month was over of our cute, sweet and my first ever relationship! If I was asked for a wish from God, I would definitely ask for her cause I was in the centre of a pool-filled with Love and my eyes was not ordinary any more. It was like the DSLR camera which only focused on girl, named her and everything else seemed blur.

We shared gifts and then I realized that I was stupid and an idiot fellow! Seriously guys you won't believe I gifted her nothing other than chocolates at the end of the first month of our relationship.

We met at our common place with Bhavesh. Firstly, I opened my bag and removed one Kit Kat, then a dairy milk, then a Kit Kat, it was going on and she was shocked and waiting for me to say "yes now chocolates are over."

After this stupidity, she opened her bag and gave me a gift, it was covered with red sparkling wrapper and it was written 'Best wishes and happy anniversary.' My hands were not able to destroy the gift packing to remove the gift and she was waiting for me to remove the gift from the wrapper! 'Remove it fast' she said with an expression of irritation and I did it.... It was a wallet she introduced all the things to me from "A TO Z" and I was just smiling at her. "THAT WAS THE BEST FEELING IN THE WORLD."

We were looking at each other and Bhavesh removed his bag from his shoulder! We asked together, you too bought a gift for us? He was smiling and gave us a wonderful gift. It was a sketch of me and Nency from the photo which we clicked at cafe coffee day. In that photo we were drinking our favourite coffee 'Crunchy Frappe' from one glass and we both were looking at each other surprisingly when Bhavesh said that he had created that sketch by his own.

"LIFE IS TOO SHORT COLLECT MEMORIES"

I was not able to throw that gift wrapper so that wrapper was with me for a long time in good condition and I used that wallet too in my routine life also that sketch was with me before the things got messed up.

"No matter how much you argue with that one person over little things, ultimately you love him/her exactly for what they are. None of those expensive gifts or sweet words and chocolates meant anything if one can't appreciate the little things that matter."

"Best day of your life is when you give up on everything you are surrounded with and just think of only one-person whole day I must say everyone on this earth should fall in love once it is great feeling I ever had."

CHAPTER 7

In the middle of sea named love

4 July 2016,

"OUT OF CITY AND FAR FROM HEADACHE"

I often visit a small village named, Motimarad, near the popular town Dhoraji, my maternal grandpa and grand mom stayed there. I felt free and independent there so, I was there for fun and refreshment.

Some of my best buddies lived there (Dhruvi, Deep Bhai, Nishadi) they are cousins and best friends. I share my personal stuff with them mostly just because of them I like Motimarad.

Night out, fun, food, craziness (Me, Dhruvi, Mohil, Megha di) on the roof top talking about each other and irritating others. I left Dhruvi's home at 4:30 and plugged my charger in and slept uncommonly.

5 JULY 2016,

"INTIMACY STARTS HERE"

The day when I felt like I did it something that was missing from the beginning, we bunked our class and went on a long drive at our common place @new ring road.

I think everyone should keep special places for different things they did and the pagal ladki Amber taught me to have one place to visit when you become sad, it controls your emotions and gives you answers of all your questions.

10 JULY 2016,

"FIRST TIME, THE GIRL ON MY BULLET"

-ISHVARIYA POST

We were not having classes and we came to know that when we reached the class, I borrowed Parth's bike and gave it to Bhavesh to join us and we moved on my bullet. I was enjoying her company. Here we go! #bullet@100km/h new ring road she was shouting at me all the way.

We reached Ishvariya and met her friend. She was enjoying with her bf and it was fixed for them on weekends. We found sanctum and I showered flowers of romance on her when Bhavesh was finding something to eat.

Love gives you happiness as like a thirsty man feels by having a glass of pure and sweet water from the salty ocean.

I was enjoying each second of my life. Days moved like metro and nights with her dreams. Now that was what I was waiting for. I found new world in her. In fact, she was my world I wish we could have that days back but that was not possible at all.

16 JULY 2016,

"I DON'T LIKE TO BE WET BUT ITS FINE I'M IN LOVE"

Usually, I don't like to move out anywhere in rain but I like to do everything for her which another boy could refuse.

We left the class. It was pouring and she asked me for a long drive. I had never denied any of her decisions and

31

choices till that day. We went on a drive and I was feeling cold. She was rubbing my hand to make me feel good, that was an awesome drive and I suffered from cold due to that but I felt that was nothing in return of that smile on her face.

30 JULY 2016,

"TWO MONTHS OVER"

I don't know how those days passed and how my leg slipped each day deep in her love. It was like having a small diamond from a treasure and having satisfaction all along that. No more dreams other than that, no more hope from another people, nothing other than that one person you rely on!

As usual I was late and we were supposed to reach the class early but again Bhavesh always remained a reason for it. We were going to buy a gift for her and we were roaming in the mall at around 9 O' clock like terrorists. Finally, we got a gift for her "Think, Pink, and Bling T-shirt" and one Fogg from Bhavesh. We called her and gave her a surprise at back side of the class and we moved into the library to focus on main goal i.e. "IELTS."

Two months were over and there was a bond and intimacy between us we trusted each other like a baby trusts his/her parents. I had no words for that relationship. I didn't leave any excuses or any mistakes. Even I don't think I left anything which she wanted from me. I gave my 100% but vo kehte hena "mohabat bhi zaruri thi bichhadna bhi zaruri tha."

I never thought that it may be one sided love but it was not. There was a time when I felt that and even I believed that it was one sided love. I didn't know what it was but it was better than today and I will never forget those days. I will never have that happiness and that passion in my love again! Never, doesn't matter how good anyone loves me (she proved me wrong! guess who was she?)

7 AUGUST 2016,

"Friendship day"

We were not able to meet on the Friendship day. She was sleeping because she had a night out with her family at her home and I thought we will meet but unfortunately! Well it was not the Valentine's Day so it was all okay.

I thought I was utilizing my precious time with the people who were going to hold my hand at my worst but everyone knew "kismat badi kutti chiz hoti he..." they left me just like that and I got too many people who still held my hand and say "it's alright" so, yes, I was still happy after that spark even today I didn't have any regrets about what decisions I took in past. I knew I was right but yes, I missed that moments of my life I lived with her and I miss her too. I wanted to tell her one thing 'yes I am talking about Nency' She hurt me and that was the worst days of my life each minute of that days was like one whole year for me. It was past and I just wanted to go on with that flow. I was happy that I was living my life. I had new friends, new mates, who would never leave me alone and never hurt me like she did. "SORRY NENCY, AND BIG THANKS TO OTHER PEOPLE WHO HELPED ME IN MY TOUGH SITUATION" (special thanks to the two stars of my life 1st one was always AMBER and another one was Megha, a good friend of mine, who was always supportive and the girl with whom I could go completely crazy, she held me, guided me when it was not my cup of tea. Apart from Megha and Amber, Preeti, meet Monik, Keyur, Bhavesh, Harshit and many more supported me a lot.)

CHAPTER 8

Dissatisfaction 9/10

23 August 2016

"JANMASHTAMI"

Yes, that was the only thing we could do, "long drive" #fun, outing, bullet350, our place, love, joy, trust, honesty overspread! That day we enjoyed a lot. We packed some snacks with us and moved to our place, we were talking with each other and I said her a line "Nency, everything is like a dream, you and me alone." Yes, that day I was feeling different. The environment we were enjoying was like a dream but it was a reality.

I was wondering that my life was no more boring. It was completely entertaining and full of romance. I was smiling internally thinking that 'yes finally I got the partner' who would be with me no matter what happens. Those types of thoughts gave me more happiness, my world was then around some selected people who were the reason for my new step in new life. Definitely it was a new world to me because I never thought of loving someone.

24 August 2016

"One of the wonderful day."

"Yes, I agree guys, pyar ma insan pagal ho jata he... lekin vo pyar hi kya jisme pagalpan na ho!" I don't know what was that feeling? I was confused seriously. She sent me screenshots of the current movie shows and zoom... I wore my clothes, raincoat, started my bike and went for a movie with her in heavy rain! I hate getting water on my body and clothes except when in the bathroom, then also I went with her. I mean even when my cousins forced me to go crazy in rains I was like 'no you enjoy it's not my cup of tea' but the feeling that provoked me to go was different. I was not at all interested in a ride or a movie I was just excited to have some good time with her of course she was the one I was mad for.

The story was not over there! We had a "Coca Cola" and we were totally wet! and omg! The AC of that bloody theatre cold enough to spoil a movie.

Next day morning "FEVER"

30 September 2016

"4 months over! Gift for her! Again, dissatisfaction and loss of feelings."

I bought a massage box for her and her excuse was how to keep that with her and she denied to keep it by saying it's impossible to take that home! I could run for her to bring water or to bring tea. I could move fast to reach for the class with her. I could wait hours for her on WhatsApp. I could take her with my parents at funfair. I could move in heavy rain on bike about 20 km just because she asked for a movie. I could go with her on a long drive in rain even if I was suffering from cold and she just couldn't keep a small gift which contained lots of love and feelings????

"Seriously I felt very bad on that day but I didn't disclose. It was also my fault."

As per her wish I asked my mom and sisters to join us at "Aaradhya club presents Navratri " and I did everything she said. There was not even one incident when I said "NO I CAN'T!!!"

At that day she was so happy and I've never realized that she will behave rude at that level but she did and I accepted again and again not because she was my girlfriend just for the love in which I was falling a bit more day by day.

At one point of I time thought that she was not in love with me but I ignored and internally decided that she was just confused about our relation and a hangover of her first boyfriend, Arjun was still annoying her. Yes, she had a boyfriend and I was always single in search of my true love. She thought I didn't know anything but trust me I was more famous, more intelligent, more powerful and richer than her shitty boyfriend, Arjun. I got all her stuff and I always knew that she was lying to me. I even knew her personal stuff with him. The more I reveal, the more it would hurt, so let it be. The things I heard from my friends and cousins were unbelievable I thought they were feeling jealous and they were having problem to digest that she was my girlfriend but all of them couldn't lie. I knew after my breakup, each word which Monik and Deep bhai had informed me was 100% true.

In the middle of my ordinary life after small breakups, she was not satisfied so a big blast in the days of Navratri. After the first day of Navratri, she changed her behaviour, that was the time when she thought that she loved Arjun, not me but I disclosed each and everything and she kept it all as a secret. I didn't even know that she had a boyfriend in the past. I got news from my friends and that's the worst thing which could happen in any boy's life. We were standing outside in the parking after class me, Bhavesh and Nency! It was raining slowly. The sky was dark and full of cloud. She was speaking in English with me and she said that she didn't love me. My life took a pause at that moment for a second, I felt like someone was snatching her from me. I reacted normal although it was tough to smile and stay cool without uttering a word. Few days later, before Dussehra, our batch had a party at Ghanteshvar park which was organized by Shivani ma'am, our IELTS practice batch faculty, I must say, the leader of our team. That time my days ended with reading love stories, listening breakup songs and asking her, actually begging her for love, everyone asked me repeatedly what happened and I was in my own life and trying more and more for her. I was at my home everyone was going for a party and I was just listening songs at home, crying internally but my mom asked me couple of times what happened to me, I was are not shinning like my star." Mom said me to go to Ghanteshvar and be refreshed but I denied cause I wanted to be alone even I wanted to meet her and ask her that why couldn't we stay together! Everyone was enjoying TV.

Keyur came beside me and said, "Let's move to Ghanteshvar." He knew my silence.

I said, "No," and after few seconds I said, "Come on let's go." We said to mom that we were going to Shivshakti for enjoyment and we reached Ghanteshvar, moved in, the security asked for entry fee! Hell! F*** off man we moved in by saying that we knew the owner and we really did. He was my dad's friend. We moved in and suddenly at the edge of the garden, we found them. All of them were sitting in round shape and talking with each other. They greeted me with 'Hi' and Keyur took a chair far from us because he was an unknown there. I took my place and Hitesh asked me if he was Keyur? I replied, "Yes" and he moved near Keyur. Ma'am asked me, "Why you didn't come with us?" and I said, "Look at me ma'am I am in night dress. My friend is at my home for the weekend, how can I come to you guys without him and if I would ask him to join us he would deny cause he wanted to stay with me at my home."

Few minutes later they started truth and dare and was waiting for her to talk to me in personal but I hesitated to ask and Keyur shouted my name and I said all of them that I was going 'bye.' After that we were waiting for her to reply but she was not answering my call and ignoring my text. Finally, she came at the entrance and Keyur left us all alone to talk freely. I asked her, "Why are you doing like this?" And then she replied me with some harsh words said me that she didn't love me and our parents will not accept our relation, that didn't mean we had to leave each other. I tried to explain him at last. Tears came rolling down from my eyes and at that time Keyur came to me and said, "Let's go."

Bhavesh and Keyur tried to explain her about my feelings and she said the worst thing ever 'you should not speak that Nency, you don't have any right to do so' she said that she did not liked nature of my mom. Keyur said, "Say something or let me speak or else let's just move out." And we went home lastly. She said she would stay with me and said sorry for the words that hurt me.

I thought it was alright and everything will go perfect but no! I was wrong, she again started ignoring me and my calls, started enjoying herself with her group I hated when she gave my place to Hitesh in her life. I didn't have any problem with Hitesh but once I hated him a lot. It was like I was watering a plant every day and he snatched the flowers from the plant before I smelled it and even he enjoyed the smell of that flower in front of me.

CHAPTER 9

Messed-up things

I accepted it was a breakup.

Days went off I started finding my love in novels and found myself in every guy who was in breakup mode and remembered the days we spent together in love. I gave her and at last 2-3 tears with a question that why? If she didn't want a serious relation, why she played with my feelings? I did every foolish thing which a guy does after breakup - living alone, listening music, ignoring friends, bunking class, sleeping a lot, reading books, writing a diary, planning for suicide, and much more. She ignored my texts and me in class. I tried to make her feel that I loved her a lot but she was firm in her decision that she did not love me and even she also said she was never in love with me.

She kept maintaining a distance between us and people were wondering about the distance we created between us, from together in one bench to opposite parts of the class and conversation changed its way from 'let's go for a ride to lets go home,' from 'I will not leave you alone to leave me alone,' 'from call me now to call me later,' 'from I am free to I don't have time,' 'from take care to I don't care,' 'from I love you to I don't!'

From the beginning of my relationship I was not in contact with Amber but after my breakup, she came like a cold-water shower in hot dessert and before that my school friend Megha was the person to figure out my problems and make me feel that it's alright nothing strange had happened so keep calm and focus on your goals. Before everything happened, our chair was fixed in the library, one table was fixed for three of us me, Nency and Bhavesh. They were having exams together and I was also having my exams in the same month so again places in the library changed along with the relationship status. Before breakup we used to call each other, meet in the backyard of class and move to the class together but then she started calling Hitesh and I stopped calling everyone. I have waited for her even at 7 O clock in the morning to give her a Kit Kat but she ruined everything. When a baby gets a new toy, old toys becomes boring. Even if the old one gave more happiness, the new one becomes interesting. Same thing was happening with me.

One day after a fight at the backside of the class in front of Keyur and Bhavesh, I bunked the class and called Keyur. We met at Indira circle and I accepted that it was a breakup and I should move on but it was difficult for me to accept that "Nency" whom I loved the most left me alone and behaved like nothing had ever happened between us. Even an eye contact between us became rare but I accepted that she would never come back to me no matter how hard I try.

I stopped looking at her and started ignoring her. I was missing her lot looking at our photos in laptop, hearing old call recordings, crying in bathroom and acting like I didn't care. It is greatly believed that if you got some bad time in your life you will definitely have good time ahead and if you can't get it done, something more worth might be waiting for you. Yes, back to cutie pie Amber, whenever she was in touch with me, I was single when I started IELTS and then after breakup. Nency started her practice with Hitesh and to show everyone that it was alright and I didn't care. I started practising with Amber, Preeti and Sanjay. I was in depression and I got someone who could try to understand my feelings. She was Preeti I texted her my whole story and she guided me what to do ahead (thanks a lot dear for giving me a new life if I am something in my life, the credit goes to the two angels of my life, Preeti and Amber.) Finally, our group was divided, but Bhavesh was common in both groups. I started my same old life in a new group and set a goal that I would achieve 6.5 bands with no less than 6 in each module. Preeti helped me in the library and Amber entertained me couple of times during practice. We heard songs in the library and acted like we were practising listening module.

Finally, the exams knocked the door of all of us turn by turn. I wished her good luck in the early morning. She was speaking as if she was not interested. I wrote something on the wrapper and gave it with chocolate but she was busy with Hitesh even then. I had a self-respect, I moved back saying that I need to go to pick up my brother and Sanjay, Hitesh and Bhavesh, moved inside with her. Turn by turn, the exam was over and everyone was waiting for the results.

I moved to Motimarad (my maternal parents' home) after completing my exams and the time I spent with her on phone calls was same as it was before breakup just the name had changed. Before it was with her and now it was with Amber. I gave Amber, a couple of surprises in which Chintan, my school friend played a role of my buddy who delivered her the food parcels. We were having good time knowing each other and I always kept in mind that she was engaged so there was no chance and even I never thought about her in that manner she motivated me to get rid of my breakup mode to forget my ex and move on. Suddenly Nency changed the conversation and way of speech, she was behaving normal and trying to get close again. She asked me to join her and Bhavesh at Dominos. I denied and I informed Amber that she was talking like that in phone calls and Amber knew that finally I was out of all that silly things which I did after breakup and she didn't want me to get back into that because she knew how hard it was to take me out of that, she clearly said me, "No Darshit, no matter what happens but please don't say yes if she is going to propose again. And if you want to say yes than you can but I will never talk to you and move away from your life forever."

I was crying and thinking that I trusted Nency once and then it was turn to trust Amber so I put the call down and after few seconds Nency called me. She tried to push me on the track of our relation and I changed the topic repeatedly. Even that day she was trying to make me feel jealous by informing me about that chats of her with Hitesh. I remembered the words of Amber and continued for about an hour on call but I did not move to the track she wanted me to go and even not said a 'yes' for joining her at the Dominos.

Two days later I came back home and finally said "yes" for Dominos just because of Bhavesh. We ate pizza's and we were moving back to home after all those things happened between us. She wanted nothing between us and then she tried to create something and again she was speaking about Arjun without anyone asking. I never asked her about him even I said her not to take his name in front of me and Bhavesh also never asked her about him. Then also she started that 'we used to do this, we used to do that, we used to talk under that tree and all that,' actually that didn't matter anymore, so, I moved back to home after having dinner and had a great sleep even after her daily soap.

CHAPTER 10

No love no story

After couple of days, Preeti said, "Let's meet at SS Food Zone."

I was ready as always. I informed Bhavesh and he asked Nency to come. She thought only three of us were going to meet. I was really feeling good but each second, I heard her name I moved in flashback for a while. I was waiting for her with Bhavesh at the SS and she came, took a seat and started playing with her mobile, she knew everything about me, my likes, my dislikes and truly she never skipped a chance to show off with the stuff related to Arjun. It was the time of Demonetization. Our Prime Minister demonetized currency notes of Rs. 500 and Rs. 1000 and Arjun posted a photo on social media with bundles of notes in which he acted like he was feeling what to do? And with that photo she showed off a lot. I was not at all interested in her talks and the things she was doing just to make me feel jealous. She swiped another photo and said see he has the same jacket like me! What the hell! I was feeling so much confused and I thought I need to take revenge. I called psycho(Amber), "Where are you? I'm waiting here at SS."

She asked, "Sanjay and Preeti are coming?"

I said, "Yes, they are on the way. You come fast I'm waiting here."

Nency was wondering whom I called, she asked Bhavesh, "Who is coming?" And I said, "Amber is coming and she stood up, took her mobile and wallet and said, "I'm going I'm already late," and Bhavesh was fighting with her and requesting her to stay and lastly Bhavesh gave her key of her Activa. She was about to leave and at that second Preeti and Sanjay entered in. She didn't have a choice finally, Amber was yet to come and I was waiting for her to take the revenge.

Finally, everyone was there and Preeti baked a cake for us and we ordered ice cream and I started enjoying with Amber to make her feel jealous. Amber was not at all aware about why I was doing so but she was innocently reacting to me as usual. I played music in my laptop she denied and Bhavesh was also feeling annoying but Amber supported me. Amber treated me ice-cream from her spoon and that was the perfect revenge. I was in the deep thoughts of how she was creating a scene by showing me photos of Arjun and something happened. I don't know how but I slapped Amber! She started crying and I moved towards her saying her sorry again and again, everyone else moved down stairs along with Nency and Bhavesh that was not important for me I just wanted Amber to stop crying and say it's ok but Preeti and Amber too went downstairs. It took time to hear its ok from Amber but lastly, she forgave me. I still feel sorry for that moment. (Sorry Amber)

Amber was the only one who was repeatedly trying to push me back on track and she exactly knew what I was feeling. On the other hand, I was not in touch with Megha. If she was there, it would be easy for her to throw me back to my life far from sadness but Thank God, she was not there. If she was the story would be over even before starting.

I went to Bharat tea stall near Akashvani circle with Bhavesh where Hari provided us with tea (Hari was a boy working at Bharat tea stall.) It was the common place for us to refresh ourselves. I knew she would create a scene and again she'd start blaming me. She texted me "don't call me and text me by" I replied "ok." I was feeling so much stressed. I mean what the hell I was totally collapsed down in sadness. My feeling was like I was not able to control myself and not even ready to tell anyone. As I wrote before It was the time of Demonetization. Currency notes of Rs. 500 and Rs. 2000 were replaced with the new ones, I needed Rs. 500 new notes. I asked Bhavesh and he informed Nency. She asked both of us to meet at backyard of class. I knew that currency notes were not the exact reason to meet. She wanted to argue with me and she wanted to blame me for the things that happened at SS Food Zone. I did not want to break her heart so I was afraid to meet her but I didn't have any option left. Currency notes were as important as my relationship was with her. We took an auto and moved towards the class and waited for her. She came like a hurricane and provided notes to Bhavesh. It was not over just like that. She started firing me out by her words and trust me she spoke the words that killed me every second after that. She reacted like I was just creating a mess from the last four months. I was a criminal from her side and she was a judge to punish me from my side. I was an innocent, still I didn't utter a word before it was not in my hands to control my emotions. Point one - "you never loved me", point two "Arjun still loves me and that's called love" (if she argued with me like that, my words would be like 'toh uske saath hi kyun nhi rehti', point three "Amber is a characterless girl and don't act like you loved me go and sleep with her" that was enough for me to leave the place and allow my tears to roll down through my eyes. I left both of them without uttering a word because I knew that she had crossed the limits and it was my turn to do that bullshit. I started walking towards the main road. They both tried to stop me but their efforts were meaningless. I took an auto and called my mom and dad to take me from the next circle. They picked me up and Bhavesh was repeatedly trying to call me and I ignored (he always tried to push us back on track but that day it was not anyone's cup of tea because it was matter of Amber, my queen). Dad stopped the car to have some food and they went outside. Mom asked me to join them and eat something at least. I clearly denied and it was time for my tears to get out of my eyes which was partly red and full of emotions. In that time, I was hanging up call from Bhavesh and ordering him to call me next day. I thought it was Bhavesh but that time she called me. I picked up "Hello" yes speak out I said, "Sorry" hmm "just hmm?" I said its "ok" "speak out heartily" I can't I said and that's it. I thought It was all over life was ruined I was all alone no one was there for me to hold me and say "It's ok, don't worry, I was wrong."

"You'll never know the reason behind the people leaving you alone and hurting you repeatedly. Maybe the only reason is someone who is eagerly waiting for the place they occupied in your heart"

CHAPTER 11

Second half

Someone said and too many people believed 'when one door closes another opens itself for no reason' just like she left me for no reason. Now I was independent. I had wings and the sky too. I got many people who believed in me, one of them was Amber. Amber was with me all day from the morning to evening and at nights she was in my nightmare, she was more than a friend and not a girlfriend, people doubted and we kept ignoring them. Our company was like when clouds met sky, angels met stars, rain drops met sand and roads met destination. We were together for no reason, for no reason we cared for each other we felt jealous when someone else tried to create a raw between us but after all we had a blind trust on each other which provoked us to go completely crazy. I always kept a raw between both of us as I knew that she was engaged but before and after all of us there was some divine force trying to push us in the story which was decided before our birth.

Meet was our partner. Now time changed everything in a fraction of second. After breakup, Nency's place was captured by Amber and instead of losing his place Bhavesh continued with the same nature. Things changed, time changed but Bhavesh didn't. Meet (meet) was now third person of a hilarious triangle which included me and Amber. Things between three of us was going with an ease. No one was trying to hurt each other, no one was trying to ignore each other. I must say I was back to my life with that same flow but flashbacks were still wobbling around my mind at least once a day which was enough to spoil the mood of Amber and me at a time but Amber always tried to make me feel good by silly jokes and cute talks even when it was useless I felt like heaven most of times.

"Dil tha pighal gaya,

Wada tha toot gaya,

Insaan tha badal gaya,

Waqt tha guzar gaya."

Days later, again when I was not at all interested in loving anyone to that extend after that things happened my life, Nency again tried to enter in my life but it was too late. She lost me long ago, she asked me and I denied without thinking for a second I was firm at my decision and I knew what I was doing so there was nothing to regret about.

"It is like first you look for a Kit Kat and you throw it in a desire to have a temptation and again you look for the same Kit Kat which was already taken by someone else as you kicked it off from your life!"

Time changes but it takes time, I believe, Nency was out of my life and the Amber was now the centre of attraction. We had fun in our own me and Amber were doing foolish things which people hated and the meet was our leader who always gave us instructions and smashed his anger on our mischief and even motivated us when it was as necessary as words in books, pen in a diary and a zip in jeans. He was elder than both of us and experienced person in each phase of life but we were still behaving childish so we just laughed at him. All in all, I should say it was more fun having Amber as a friend than Nency as a girlfriend.

All of us knew that the days we were living together was going to be an unforgettable memory and last couple of days were left to have fun together but no one was aware about the things that were happening between me and Amber, we both were each other's best mate and fun partners. I never thought what would I feel when she would move far from me but I enjoyed the life she gifted me. I must say she had her right on my life because I was lost somewhere else and she took me out of it and taught me what love was in actual life and how should we react to it. Even after many thoughts, many lessons many, mistakes people fall in love. I mean how was that possible once you know that the thing that hurts you, fall again. Get rid of that bullshit and never give space to such things in your life I started believing, I was firm at my decision that I would not fall in love again. Meet always gave me true advice and I completely agreed but for one sentence I never agreed with him until it happened to me that was: "In life you will have at least one girl with whom you will be enjoying your time and you will keep in mind that no I can't love her and I will not love her no matter what happens but you will fall in love again."

Now life was simple yet complex. For me it was simple for the people who had all the knowledge of relations, love stories and life were complex. The people who were aware about my future were warning me repeatedly to take care "love badi hi kamini chiz he kisi se bhi kabhi bhi ho skta he." I was confident enough to answer all. It was like when you clear one level you think you got all the tricks to win the game. At least once in a day someone gave me an indirect advice to not to fall in love with Amber. I was internally confirmed with my heart that I will never fall in love again even, not with my wife and I always explained that to my friends too that don't worry between me and Amber, its nothing more than a friendship and they again warned me that with any other girl it's not an issue but in case of Amber it was like we all were scared because she was again of my caste and she was engaged and her marriage was about to come so if we would do something without thinking, it would ruin our life completely. So, in my life, love had no space and I was happy with the feeling that Amber gave me, so there were zero possibilities of love between me and Amber.

CHAPTER 12

Arrange marriage

Amber was getting married and I was not having any trouble with that. The thing which irritated me was that what if she would forget me and get busy with her married life, so, I decided to visit her marriage function even when I knew that it could lead to a big trouble for all of us but my heart was not ready to skip that very important part of her life. I wanted a good memory of her marriage to be with me forever. During that phase, I accepted that she would forget me and will not be able to contact any of us, so, that became reason for my sadness.

I was ready to go and moved to The Grand Murlidhar near my home hotel and night out place for teenagers by Abhal Bhai Kuvadiya, he was the owner at that place and we held a good relation since years so I had a small talk with him and moved to the chair. I was eagerly waiting for Meet to come. He said that we both were going to her marriage. I was looking here and there and my eyes stuck at a car at the parking. I guess he was Meet. Unfortunately, not due to heavy traffic in the city, he came late and I was sure that he would make an excuse that it was late, so we should drop the idea, he was right at his own because we were supposed to drive about 2 hours, that too in the dark. He came, took a chair and we started discussing pros and cons of attending the marriage of a best friend.

Finally, we moved inside the car to start our journey. We ate "masala pan" to refresh ourselves and moved in. Meet started car, unlocked the handbrake and instead of gearing up he was lost somewhere else. Few seconds later he said, "Let me think by the brain of Meet, 25 years old. Meet, not Darshit who is just 18 years old." I got his point and at last after discussing a lot we dropped our idea. He dropped me near my home and moved to his home to get his mind refreshed he was looking more stressed than me.

I thought I would not be able to see her again so it was the last option for me to look at her, beyond limits and that too was gone wrongly planned. If I had Keyur with me instead of Meet, it would be 100% possible and even 100% dangerous.

CHAPTER 13

Million Dollar Businessman

Life started with new goals and new people. I started hating her day by day and that was one of the best thing I did in my life apart from loving and caring too much.

The thing I hated most about Nency was her show-off attitude. She never skipped a point of showing off but I wanted to thank her for that. It burned each part of body internally and after breakup, it created a big flame in me to earn more than her family income. It was difficult for me as I was not capable to arrange finance and even I was not having that support from my family I understood their views, they always said that I was too small to develop a business. I agreed, but I never wanted to go slow not in life and also not on roads. I had fear in me that if I'll go slow others would push me back.

I decided I want to earn more than her family income and I was sure that I would do it anyhow. I had to do any business and anything. I just started to look for the opportunities. One person I trusted at that time was Keyur, my friend forever. I knew that he will help me for anything so I kept his name in my mind for finance now. Next thing was to think about a job or business. After setting up my business I could easily go for a job but after job I couldn't get into business so first option I locked - first business then job. Next question was which business? I knew that all the fame, money, property, everything me and my father had was due to my grandfather and how he earned all these was a good point for me. He earned all of these with the business of stone mine digging out stones and selling it. Also taking river banks on lease from the government and selling sand. Most sand in our city was provided by him. All in all, I knew that money which I want was in the field of building materials.

I often visited our stone mine which was about 10km from my home. It was big and always full of water because it had been years, we stopped digging out stone. The rain water got collected in it. Whenever I visited that place I always thought why my family members is not doing anything with that place it was so big and there were many opportunities to earn good money. One day I was sitting there and had an idea of utilising the water from it. I had 2 things to do - sell water which was not drinkable or utilise it for other purposes. After few minutes, an idea flicked through my mind. It was about how to utilise water and sand which came from rivers were always dirty and included part of small particles of sand but it should not contain that amount of small particles so they shower water on truck full of sand and push a pipe inside the sand on the truck and start the diesel engine to throw out water from the pipe to the truck with great force which cleaned all sands and small particles which were of no use and came out of the truck with water and clean sands remained in it. It took around one hour to wash one truck of sand and people charged Rs. 350 per truck. I thought if 10 trucks would come, it would be Rs. 3500 and if we remove 1000 as a part of expense, we could earn Rs. 2500 daily even when the sand was washed, some of good and cleaned sand also came out of truck which was about 1 truck every 10 days which could be easily sold out for 4 to 5000 so it could be a golden business for me I thought and started dreaming about other things.

Then, the final step was finance. The business was good enough to make me earn more than a family income but what about investment? I knew my dad was not going to support me and I believed that my mom would do. Moved home and bombarded my feelings to start that business. They shouted on me but finally they agreed and said to collect information about the diesel machine which we were going to place on that stone mine. Partner in crime, partner in business more than a friend Keyur, I called him and said everything I had in my mind he just asked me one question, "How much money you need?" I said, "I don't know let's first collect information about the machine." I was not able to do that also so I asked Keyur to arrange that. He moved to the shops with our common friend Hiren Mori. They sent me clicks in WhatsApp and it was about Rs. 20000. It was so less as compared to the income but it was not my cup of tea at that time to arrange that alone. Even pipes and other stuff was of about Rs. 3000, so we need around Rs. 25000 to start up that business. I asked for money to my mom and dad. Mom gave me her personal savings of Rs. 4000 and dad gave nothing other than dirty looks at first but how could he resist himself not giving a single penny, so, he gave me Rs. 5000 new notes which smelled awesome it was Rs. 9000 then. Everything else depended on Keyur. He arranged 10000 and we moved to buy the machine after bargaining a lot. At last we bought the machine for Rs.18500 which was of Rs. 20000 and then it was time to go for it. I moved to the stone mine with the machine. Keyur and dad came on Keyur's bike after buying oil and diesel for the machine. When we installed parts of the machine, dad bought the pipe. It took 2 to 3 hours for us to complete our work. Finally. It was getting dark then and we moved home. Even we were not able to stand up after that work but the flame of money and new business was burning in me and Keyur and dad were happy that we were doing something else than just hanging around. We thought we should take care of the machine for few days as my dad were there after many years and even people of the village were not aware about our new business so we moved to the stone mine at 11 O' clock to protect our machine from the anti-social elements which often came there and have drinking parties, thinking that no one else visited that place. We started fire and then had discussion about what to do on the next day.

The morning sun sparkled all of us. We went to the stone mine, did a pooja together and waited for the truck. The truck came, I still remember it was a yellow truck with 2233 number on the number plate. I still had that money that I earned from the first truck, with me. To stay in competition and break others business, we kept Rs. 250 per truck. It took 2 days to boost up my business in which my mom, dad and Keyur supported me a lot. It was perfect and at the age of 18 years, I was owner of my own business. It was the best moment of life for me. I just wanted to go ahead with that flow.

Days went by, we settled our business and now it was time to get something new. We visited Purva Infrastructure Company by Nilesh Lunagariya. He was the main person and our boss there. After meeting him, he became the role model of my life. I always dreamt of having a good personality and big business like him. I was there for documentation work of Rs. 10,000 salaries per month and simple work. I was not there to do a job, I was there to learn new things and expand my contacts in the 3 months of the job duration at Purva Infrastructure. I earned 30000 salaries and bought a 3bhk flat of 14 lacs on loan. All my friends and relatives argued how I would pay the instalment of Rs. 15000 per month. I had my business which gave me 30 to 40 thousand rupees per month so it was not an issue for me. Then at the age of 18, I was owner of my business and a 3bhk flat.

My dream of earning more than her family income came true and I was not going to stop myself with just couple of things, I had many ideas and things to do in my life which were of no use as my mom and dad wanted me to study further out of India. They knew that I was mad about making money which may lead to back steps in my educational career.

CHAPTER 14

Good Bye Preeti

The day everyone was waiting for was not far then. Preeti was the first person from our batch to have a visa stamp on her passport and her dreams too. She arranged to get together me Preeti, Meet, Sanjay and Hitesh met at Quiches. I was not able to control myself. I knew that I was going to miss her a lot. She was always there for me and guided me as an elder sister. It was like a family and one member was going to leave all of us but we all knew that everyone from group was supposed to leave the country one by one. I was happy that the visa was granted but sad too because she was going. She was angel of my life. Part of my new life and even she was the first person to listen my whole breakup story and guide me further. I would never forget Preeti. She shouted on me whenever I was out of control and pushed me back on track. She helped me to score good in IELTS and I know she cared my existence in her life. Lastly, I would end up my feelings by writing about her and describing her, "You are the cream of my coffee, ice of my juice, salt of my food and doctor of my mood."

CHAPTER 15

Come Back

When your mind believes in reality, your heart always makes you believe in magic. I lost Amber as she got married to the boy who was well settled and earned better than me. My mind accepted that she was not going to come back but her call after marriage forced me to believe that she was not gone yet.

I was depressed and stressed too much due to work and business pressure, failure in process of moving abroad and other problems was killing me day by day. The only option left with me to refresh myself was moving to Motimarad for the weekend. I packed my bags, booked tickets and took a window seat. I was supposed to change buses just for the last 15 to 20 km. I left the first bus and looked around for something to drink. It was hot enough to spoil my health instead of ignoring, I had a cold drink and waited for other bus in the shade.

I entered the other bus, took a seat and just when I was giving money for the ticket, my phone rang! The name that displayed was AMBERADIQUEEN. I was not able to control my emotions so I started smiling and forgot to take the money back from the conductor of bus, who gave me the ticket. I knew I should be angry with her for a long time because she was not answering any text messages in our group and calls were not allowed, she informed us before marriage.

"Hello…" she spoke!

"Where were you? you don't have time for us right? Go to hell. You might be happy without me. Even you didn't not reply to my texts in group. I know you were online and changing display pictures often. I know everything but you didn't need us, not even me!" I fired my feelings just in couple of seconds and then I was feeling free.

We continued our talks for few minutes than she hanged up may be her mother in law was there so I didn't ask for a reason for saying goodbye even when we were hearing each other's voice after a long time. I always record calls on my phone and backup daily, there was a time when I used to listen to the old recordings.

I was happy, I came to know that she still remembered me and would never forget me. When I was at the edge of believing that she forgot all the things we did together, she called me and gave life to my body. Before that call, business, money and job were the things I thought about all day.

After a few days, she moved to Junagadh to complete her studies. I was happy because that increased the chances of our meeting, but I was not sure if she would meet us after her marriage or not. For her it was like cheating with herself only both the side. She started calling all of us and we all were suffering from different problems so guided each other. Even that day we held each other's hand in worst situations.

To have a good time, I decided to stay with Keyur for few days and moved to job together. One night we were eating pizza and she called me! Instead of asking, she ordered me to visit Junagadh to meet her and Meet was going to be my partner. Me, Meet and Sanjay decided to go next morning. I was having my office at 10 O' clock and it was not my cup of tea to ask for a leave which was not going to be accepted at any cost so I decided to bunk that day. At morning 10 am, Meet and Sanjay called me, they were ready with car to pick me up I said my office that I was going to collect documents from costumer and we started our journey.

We reached there on time. I was supposed to return back before sunset. She came and I swear there was no change in her after marriage, not even in her personality. She was still a queen of madness. We had lunch together and moved to the car to drop her. She opened the door and looked at all of us as that day was the last day of her life. We all said 'goodbye' and Meet geared up the car she stood on the road and was looking towards car assuming that we would look back but no one did except me, from the window of the car. I was looking at her and she was looking at me and smiling. I was happy that we met her and had that much time together even after her marriage.

Days went by and I accepted many challenges to go Junagadh just to meet her but I was happy that she was maintaining the relations as strongly as I did. We had lot of good time but then it was difficult for us to call each other. She moved to her home and started living her life like a typical housewife. Her call was now just left in my dreams. People doubted that I was in love with her but I ignored. I didn't want anything from her just to stay by my side whenever I needed. Few weeks later, a news came to us that she was about to put her visa file, her husband went out of India after marriage and then it was her turn.

Our friendship then just remained in snap calls. I thought of magic but that time it was not possible. Her visa interview date was about to come and Meet was also having visa interview so with a dream of meeting her at Mumbai, I planned for Mumbai with Meet. Packed my bags and reached Mumbai and waited for her text.

CHAPTER 16

True love never dies because it always waits

Meet gave his visa interview and to refresh himself we moved to the club with our friends. Everyone was enjoying, dancing and I was thinking about Amber as she was about to leave the country few days later. She was texting me on snapchat and with each answer, my heart had a hard beat that shivered my body, my mind was distracted to her. That time it was final that she would leave all of us and would not come back. I thought that after moving out of India she would be busy with her own life and would not be able to contact me. Fear of losing her was killing me each second so I was waiting for her visa date just like I was waiting for Meet at the time of her marriage because I wanted to see her for the last time.

Now it was not possible for me to stay in Mumbai. My mom and dad were waiting for me. I packed my bags. I thought I had replaced myself with my dad on business for limited time but he had his own work, so, I didn't have any choice. I moved back to Rajkot thinking that how unlucky I was.

She gave visa interview and it was accepted. I wanted her to go abroad but not without meeting me properly and clearing the things between us. We were not able to clear things on calls or face to face, so, we needed to do it on snapchat.

She texted me "Oye you will never forget me, right?"

"I mean I wanted to say that you are leaving me alone I'm still here for you always and in all ways." I replied.

Undefined silence scattered between us with my text. I wanted some promises and she wanted to make sure that to what extent I supported her.

"Don't worry I'm always with you and I'll never leave you alone, I can do anything for you." I texted.

After few backspaces and typing she sent me a message that sparkled me up "What you can do for me? Will you marry me?" she texted. I was sure about my answer hence I said, "Yes, just tell me when and where?" Again, big silence.

We both were not proposing each other, not even dated each other, the thing we wanted was each other's hand to hold at our worst. She never committed like a relationship, not even I did, but we committed our love towards each other, love which was unconditional. I knew she was married, she would not come back to my life, then also I loved her beyond limits. In our life, we all have that one person whose words means everything for us. If he/she said it's a night we would accept it. If he/she said it's a day we would accept it. That one person in my life was Amber. I never thought of loving anyone after Nency broke my heart but I was always finding true love! which appreciated what I give and supported me how I did. I found my heaven in Amber and I was afraid of losing her but I was sure about her love towards me. She was my cupcake not my girlfriend and not just friend.

The day came when she was about to go. She texted "I am going, don't cry and I'll contact you, wait for me!" She was having her flight at 3am so I said that I'll be online to talk to her for the last time but she said, "I don't have enough battery in my phone so please don't wait for me." I didn't want to sleep but due to load of work at business, my body was not able to continue working. I was dreaming about the things that might happen and I slept. I woke up just after ten minutes when she became offline. I was sure that she would text me and I read…

"Oye wake up!!! Please I'm going …"

"Hello..."

"Darshit…"

Amber tried to call…

Eight missed calls from Amber (snapchat showed)

"Yaar please wake up"

"Okay fine I'm going now, don't text me I'll contact you soon, bye take care…"

Before she left the country, she informed me that I had to complete my degree and move ahead of depression and do something new in my life. I promised her that I'd do my best to move abroad and she also said not to fight with my mom and dad for anything she was giving me advice like she was not going to come back in my life again at any cost not even in snap calls.

The chapter was over when she was gone. I was about to forget her and my 2am friend Megha burned a flame of hope in me that she would not forget me and I should trust the love we shared. Days flew like seasons. Some days I remembered the old days, some days I was busy with business and some days just in a hangover of Amber. After exactly 23 days, when she left the country, she had a video call which was for the last time when I had a fear of losing her. I was sure that she would not forget me and our love would always shine like the full moon.

Two messages for two girls of my life:

Yaad aa raha he koi, yaad kr raha hoga koi, jiska tha intezar vapas aa raha hoga vahi! door na ho jaye ye dard teri judai ka ek vo hi to he jisme zikr tera baar hota he.

Hua he majboor aaj ye dil apni dastan sunane ko!

bewajah jal rahe honge kuch log mehfil me chiragon ki tarah.